Middlebury College

The Kaleidoscope

1898

Middlebury College

The Kaleidoscope
1898

ISBN/EAN: 9783337300524

Printed in Europe, USA, Canada, Australia, Japan

Cover: Foto ©Andreas Hilbeck / pixelio.de

More available books at **www.hansebooks.com**

MIDDLEBURY COLLEGE.

A SOUVENIR,

PUBLISHED BY

THE CLASS OF '98.

DEDICATED TO THE COLLEGE.

BOARD OF EDITORS.

JAMES A. LOBBAN, . . . CHIEF.
ROBERT L. RICE, . ASSISTANT.

ASSOCIATE EDITORS.

H. A. HINMAN. LUCIA E. AVERY.
FLORENCE C. ALLEN. FANNY M. SUTTON.

JOSEPH A. PECK, . BUSINESS MANAGER.
WM. H. BOTSFORD, ... ASSISTANT.
MICHAEL HALPIN, ... ASSISTANT.

RUTLAND, VT.
THE TUTTLE COMPANY,
PUBLISHERS.

CONTENTS.

EDITION LIMITED TO 550 COPIES,
PUBLISHED MAY, 1897.

For extra copies, apply to

LIBRARIAN, MIDDLEBURY COLLEGE,

    · · · Middlebury, Vt.

JOSEPH A. PECK, · · Middlebury, Vt.

JAMES A. LOBBAN, · Middlebury, Vt.

THE TUTTLE CO., · · Rutland, Vt.

PRICE, 60 CENTS PREPAID.

BY WAY OF PREFACE.

A NOVELTY usually demands an explanation, but if we have read aright the thoughts of Middlebury graduates and Middlebury lovers, our book will serve as its own explanation. There is a need for something which will combine, in a convenient and attractive form, facts concerning the history, location and advantages of our college and which will serve both as a souvenir for those who have been here and as a means of attraction for those who have not.

We would not for a moment have any one suppose that we have attempted an elaborate history of the college. Time and talent are lacking for such an enteprise. But if in a small degree we have caught the spirit of loyalty to our old college and succeeded in imprisoning some of it in our little book, we shall feel abundantly rewarded. As the centennial of Middlebury approaches, and all roads are leading to the Otter, we feel that anything, however humble, which will quicken the love that every Middlebury man has for his Alma Mater, needs no apology for its existence, and we would present our book, not in fear and trembling, but rejoicing that we can do something to help on the cause.

Although this is not a Kaleidoscope, yet we hope that it will reflect, not perhaps the changes of everyday college life, but those deeper changes which have made the college what it is. We have tried to trace the line of progress along which Middlebury has moved, so that even the most disinterested may see that ours is not a college which stands still in the consciousness of past achievement, but one which is still moving, and that forward. And yet we would recognize the achievements of the past, we would acknowledge our great debt to those men who have labored for the welfare and advancement of " the college on the hill " and to those others who have gone forth from her walls to win glory for her name.

We have had no example to follow, further than our own plans, so that there are doubtless many points which could be improved and many facts of interest which we have left out. The only other souvenir which we have been able to see, is that issued by James Clarence Harvey of the class of '81, a marvel of tasty work and literary skill; but in our work, we have started out on entirely different lines, though with that earlier souvenir as an inspiration. With this slight explanation, the class of '98 presents its souvenir, a tribute to our beloved Middlebury College.

MIDDLEBURY COLLEGE.

THREE years before the opening of the
present century, a County Grammar
School was established in the struggling little
town of Middlebury. By popular subscription,
enough money had been raised to erect a small,
wooden structure on the site now occupied by
the High School, and, shortly after, the school
began its work. But larger ideas soon entered
the minds of the early settlers; Vermont had
as yet no college. Why should not one be
founded by them? The transition from a
grammar school to a college could easily be
accomplished, and so heartily was the idea
taken up that the very next year the Records
of the General Assembly of Vermont contain
the petition of Gamaliel Painter and others,
praying for the establishment of a university
or college, stating that they were urged
thereto by an ardent desire to promote and
encourage the education of the youth of their
vicinity, and that already a large and commodious building had been provided. For
some reason or other, the petition was not
acted upon at once; twice it was brought up
only to be referred from committee to committee. But at last, in the fall of the year
eighteen hundred, the Legislature, then met
at Middlebury, took up the petition, and, by a
vote of one hundred and seventeen to fifty-one,
granted it.

On the same day, November first, a charter was issued to the President and Fel-
lows of Middlebury College, and the doors
were opened to students. Its prospects, however, were not bright. The country was new;
times were hard and many a settler had all he
could do to support his family, without contributing to such an undertaking. The State
had done nothing; no money had been
granted; not even grants of land, the favorite
gift of early times, were forthcoming. It had
given the college the right to live, but had
given it nothing to subsist upon. Its whole
wealth, building, lands, funds and all, did not
amount to five thousand dollars. "Hope"
said President Labaree, almost two genera-
tions later, "was the corner stone of the new
edifice and the benevolence of the people
and confiding trust in Providence its only
endowment." The town rallied well to the
support of the struggling institution.

With characteristic New England love of
learning and willingness to sacrifice for its
sake, the settlers gave from their own scanty
means, and undauntedly the college began,

ten students being enrolled that fall. The Rev. Jeremiah Atwater was the first President and associated with him was Joel Doolittle Esq., as tutor. The number of students gained rapidly, fulfilling the warmest hopes of its founders, and when the first class graduated, two years later, the college was already prosperous. Six years later, in the class of eighteen hundred and eight, twenty-three men took their degrees, and the need of more room was evident. Up to this time all the college work had been carried on in the little wooden structure first erected, and called East College.

THE OLD EAST COLLEGE.

This drawing is a *fac simile* of a sketch made by Samuel Everts, '28. East College was originally built in 1798 for the Addison County Grammar School. It was used for Recitation and Students' rooms until 1815, when Painter's Hall was completed, for recitation rooms until 1837, when the Chapel was completed and again for students' rooms until 1861. It was replaced by the Graded School building in 1867.

On the resignation of President Atwater, the office was tendered to Henry Davis, a well known professor at Union, and on his acceptance, plans were made for a new building and soon the college could boast of a new stone building, called North College. It was almost exclusively for dormitory use, and was considered a very remarkable piece of work, the massive stone walls being much admired and even wondered at.

Shortly after, the college was compelled to mourn one of its best friends and benefactors, Gamaliel Painter, whose industry and untiring care had done so much toward making the college possible. Not content with constant gifts during his life time, on his death he left all his fortune to the college. The next fifteen years seem to have had little worthy of note, except the twenty-fifth anniversary of the founding of the college, which was held in eighteen twenty-four and was attended by many old graduates. Twelve years later, however, an important addition was made in the shape of the present chapel, a large, stone building facing the east and, as an old report says, "containing a large room for public worship, besides recitation rooms, libraries, etc." Up to this time the college year had been divided into four terms, with only nine weeks vacation in all, the course of study being so arranged that needy students might drop out for the winter term, keep a district school, secure some money, and, returning in the spring, take up their work with but little inconvenience. This system was found to be of such help to many, that it was continued, with various modifications, for a number of years. The Commencement was held in August and, as now, attracted a large number of people, all the country about going in to witness the exercises. Of course, there was no elective system then, for in those days the student was considered incapable of choosing for himself. So he was fed upon Latin, Greek and Mathematics in endless repetition, with a little Chemistry, Rhetoric and Philosophy for three years, while in his fourth and last, he might regale himself with Locke "On the Human Understanding," Butler's Analogy, and such trifles.

The student was not expected to waste any time, consequently his hours of study were marked out with rigorous precision, such a course seeming to the officials a sure preventive of an overflow of animal spirits. Yet the records of the time and the tales of old graduates would seem to indicate that they did not always accomplish their purpose. Perhaps, sometimes, the old bell failed to give forth its warnings, or else did it with such a cracked, wearied tone, that it only excited pity in the minds of those hearing it. And surely the belfry door, with its outer side bound with iron, while its inner bears the unmistakable signs of an axe, probably swung by some freshman, now a grave, sedate man of the world, would bear witness that somehow an accident had happened to the college property, and we can perhaps imagine what was said the following day in chapel.

A few years later, the first fraternity of
national reputation was founded, and within
ten years two more were added. It has always
been Middlebury's good fortune that, despite
her small size, she can boast three fraternities,
all well known to the college world.

In the early part of the forties, Middlebury
lost much of its former prosperity. Sickness,
misfortune, and poverty in turn seemed destined to crush her; worse than all, many of
her alumni, formerly loyal, now were alien-
ated by the course of the college and advo-
cated merging her with the State University,
claiming that she had outlived her usefulness.
For a time her fate trembled in the balance,
but a few friends stood firm, by their zeal
repaired her shattered fortunes, and, under
new management, she emerged from the
clouds that had gathered so thickly about her
and once more regained her honored place.

In eighteen hundred and fifty was held the
semi centennial anniversary celebration of the
founding of the college and the spirit of Midd's
loyal alumni found ample voice in the Anniversary Poem, written by John G. Saxe, '39.
So strong was this feeling, that never again
was the idea of union raised into its former
prominence.

Ten years later, Starr Hall was built, similar in style to the other buildings and arranged
exclusively for dormitories. Its completion
marked a great revival for the college, and it
seemed as if she were once more truly prosperous. But it was not for long. The Civil War
soon burst out and her fairest hopes were shattered. Old Midd. was not backward. She
had always taught love for country and true
patriotism, and when the call for troops came,
the response was worthy of her teaching.
Man after man left her halls, not merely carried away by temporary excitement, or love
of change; but influenced by higher, loftier
motives, they gave up their own advancement,
sacrificing even life itself for the cause.

Fully one-half of her student body left, becoming directly or indirectly engaged in the
strife. The college felt the loss keenly. No
institution could pour out her men as she had
done and not be affected by it, while to crown
her misfortunes, a fierce fire swept through
her latest building, almost destroying it. But
she rallied nobly; once more raised the almost
ruined structure, and at last, the war over,
hoped for a period of renewed activity. In
this hope she has not been disappointed; not
that it has been all success, for she has had her
ups and downs, her good and evil portion, but
the general effect has been a steady march

onward. Save for the admission of women, a step bitterly opposed by many of her strongest alumni, but which was sure to come, and the introduction of a steadily growing elective system, the years up to ninety-four can show no noticeable change.

In that year, however, a large bequest made possible many much needed improvements. Painter Hall early lost its distinctively dormitory character and, with the exception of the parts devoted to the library and gymnasium, had been slowly falling into disuse. Work was at once begun on this building and new suites of rooms were fitted up, thus restoring it in part to its ancient use. A steam plant was put in operation, and the whole building renovated and repaired, the old wooden steps giving place to new ones of marble, while the much worn canopies were taken away entirely.

Within, the reading room has been enlarged, the "gym." has been greatly improved and with the addition of new apparatus, new lockers, and bath rooms, a much better opportunity is afforded the student to indulge in every sort of athletics. Class work in gymnastics has also been introduced, and has already proved its efficiency in stronger bodies and clearer minds.

The chapel, too, felt the new order of improvement. New recitation rooms, a study for the women of the college, and an enlarged, improved chapel have been the results. Steam has replaced the stove, so well known to many an alumnus, and the old wood box has become a thing of memory. On the lower floor, new laboratories, fitted up after the most improved models, show the college's growing interest in chemistry and biology, while last, but not least, a new bulletin board with glass covered front has replaced the old one, so worn with the points of countless tacks.

On the Campus, the old fence has disappeared, the little saplings of fifty years ago are tall, strong, trees, some even beginning to feel the marks of time. Waldo Avenue, with its close-locked evergreens, is no more; even the road is changed, while just across the campus stands the college boarding hall, run under student management, with the greatest success.

Starr Hall alone remains unchanged; the boys still climb the well-worn stairs, the hollows deepening day by day. Still the coal man carts his wares up the flights and the borrower with his empty hod and pleasant smile still stalks the hall.

Outwardly the change is great, but within, Old Midd. is much the same, ever striving to

give her sons and daughters a broad, firm
foundation upon which to build in after years.
Today her troubles seem over; her prosperity
is assured, and she looks forward with confi-
dence to the opening of the new century.

A NEW CENTURY HYMN.

BY PRESIDENT J. E. RANKIN, '48, HOWARD UNIVER-
SITY.

1.   We may not live to see it,
        The lips of cannon dumb!
     But the stars of Heav'n decree it,
        And it shall surely come:
     The day, war's blood-stained banner
        Shall 'neath the Cross be furled,
     And with their glad hosanna
        The nations belt the world.

  Chorus:
        We may not live to see it,
        But the stars of Heav'n decree it
           And it shall surely come.

2.   We may not live to sing it,
        Our dust may silent lie,
     But the stars of Heav'n will bring it,
        The day-dawn from on high.
     The angels have foretold it,
        In their divinest speech;
     And though ages late withhold it,
        Their anthem we shall reach.

  Chorus:
        We may not live to sing it,
        But the stars of Heav'n shall bring it,
           The day-dawn from on high.

3.   We may not live to win it,
        May die mid toils and cares;
     But the stars of Heav'n are in it,
        We'll keep it in our prayers.
     That way, time's course is steering,
        The day will come at length:
     The Son of Man appearing
        And trav'ling in His strength.

  Chorus:
        We may not live to win it,
        But the stars of Heav'n are in it,
           We'll keep it in our prayers.

COLLEGE PUBLICATIONS.

IN the same degree that literature is the re-flection and reproduction of life, is college literature the reproduction of college life. It may be likened to a mirror in which one may gaze, seeing, not always the real literary ability of the student body, but the amount of college spirit which they collectively possess.

Journalism in Middlebury College has been making vast strides in the last seventy-five years. What was then an unknown depart-ment, has now come to be one of the ruling factors in college life.

The first trace of journalism is discovered about thirty years after the founding of the college. Perhaps the necessity of some dis-tinctively college paper originated in the "University Quarterly," which was edited by the principal colleges and universities of Europe and America. At any rate, it is inter-esting to note that as the first copy of that publication was called the "Undergraduate," so Middlebury's first college paper, published Oct. 28, 1830, bore upon its title page the same word, "Undergraduate."

The origin and success of this publication was due in large measure to Jonathan Blanch-ard, of the class of '32; but even his untiring energy gave way before the problems of finance. The paper died, in full literary health and bloom, on Oct. 6, 1831, having sent out just twenty-four numbers.

The Undergraduate then was about two-thirds the size of the present one, and its pages reflected more of the knowledge of the students than it did their daily life. Long poems, historical and scientific essays make its pages appear ponderous with weight of learning. Not a trace of the jollity which then, as now, pervaded the college halls, enlivened the wise sayings. Very often the editorials were devoted to responding to the question, then puzzling the people's minds, "What is a college paper for?"

About this time we catch the echo of strange names as "Adelphi," "Shrine," "Medley," which are conjectured to be names of various college publications. But of their origin and life nothing is known.

Until 1833, the college students must have contented themselves with spouting orations as sufficient literary exercise. In that year, through the efforts of the Philadelphian and Philomathesian societies, a paper was intro-duced, known as the "Philomathesian." This might as properly be called a magazine, for

the first issue, consisting of forty pages, said:
" This work will consist of essays, occasional
reviews, comments upon new publications,
tales, poetic contributions and such disserta-
tions upon scientific subjects as shall be
deemed expedient." This first issue had eight
contributions, some of which were on the
following subjects: An essay, "Intellectual
Energy;" poems, "Mutability" and "The
Passage of the Rubicon;" fiction, "The Mad-
man's Doom" and "The Precipice" and
others of similar nature. The last issue of
this paper was in June, 1834, when it died
from lack of funds.

Then followed a long period when the jour-
nalistic spirit of the college seemed dead.
Not until 1876 was there any attempt made
by the students to record their life. Then,
through W. W. Gay, '76, the Undergraduate
again came before the public and, when making its first bow, repeated the couplet made
use of by the editor of the first "Undergrad
uate" in his opening editorial remarks:

" The good, old proverb how this pair fulfil,
    One fool is usher to another still."

From the time of its reappearance until the
present, the "Undergraduate" has been published monthly; now that it is fully established, it rests wholly with the students to
make its progress equal to that of the college.
This, then, is the extent of our strictly college
journalism, but various classes have made, at
different times, publications, which it may
be interesting to consider. In 1855 the
Sophmores first conceived of mock programs
for the Junior Exhibition. A copy of their
output, existing at the present time, differs
from the later Rams,—as these publications
came to be called,—in wholly lacking the
element of coarseness, which soon crept in,
as an almost certain accompaniment of
irresponsible, anonymous authorship. These
publications came later to be considered a
nuisance, and have been outgrown.

If the success of a paper depends upon
originality, then certainly 'Η 'ΑΦΡΟΔΙΤΗ
should be reckoned as achieving the highest
success. It was a weekly paper published by
the Class of '96 in the spring term of their
Freshman year. Its designs were wholly
original and its literary matter was certainly
refreshing for its unbounded frankness. The
reasons for editing this paper were given, in
the first number, by a member of the class
poetically inclined:

"But the Freshmen must do something;
Studies are to them but pastime,
So to please the good Professor,
Show their progress 'neath his guidance,
Set a copy for Sub-freshmen,
They resolved to print a paper."

The above quotation speaks more eloquently for the paper than words of ours would be able to.

Before the appearance of the Kaleidoscope, two editions of the catalogue were issued, one giving substantially what appears in an ordinary catalogue, and the other with the addition of pages giving the members of the various societies and fraternities. Each student subscribed for as many copies of this edition as he desired, paying his share proportionally of the cost of printing the extra pages. The college authorities paid the remainder of the expenses for printing.

In 1873, the Senior class distinguished themselves by editing the first of Middlebury's well known college annuals, "The Kaleidoscope." With ever increasing favor these have continued up to the present time, though with lamentable irregularity ; for in the twenty-three years succeeding, there appeared but fourteen annuals. In 1888 the Juniors relieved the Seniors of this task, and since that time the publishing of the "Kaleidoscope" has been a duty of the Junior class.

The editorial of that year closes with the following: "A college annual is a fragile plant, whose roots take hold on sorrow, and whose atmosphere is vexation of spirit; its sunlight is the midnight oil, it is moistened by editorial tears."

The first "Kaleidoscope" included but little more than the present catalogue, excepting mention of fraternities and clubs. But these annuals have increased both in quality and quantity, until the last issue in '95 was a volume containing much interesting literary material, copiously illustrated. Much praise is due every class producing a "Kaleidoscope," through which the alumnus can review college days, beholding the true college landscape, ever changing and varying in form and color. But the highest honor ever be to those who watched over the beginnings of these time-honored customs, breathing words of hope in times of discouragement, and fanning into still brighter flame each kindling success.

MIDDLEBURY COLLEGE IN THE WAR.

THE outbreak of the War of the Rebellion in 1861 gave rise to an excitement among the students of Middlebury College which can hardly be imagined by those who have studied there in peaceful years. Political strife had long been bitter. In the campaign of 1860, the greater part of the students favored the election of Lincoln. The Republican party up to that time had never been successful in a national contest. Lincoln's personality was almost wholly unknown. He stood for restrictions upon the further extension of slavery. The South was full of threatenings which no one believed were seriously intended. The winter following Lincoln's election was marked by repeated withdrawals of southerners from the United States Senate and other official positions; the Government seemed to be disintegrating. Lincoln was inaugurated March 4, 1861. Breaking up became more rapid; State after State passed ordinances of secession; army and navy officers went over to the South by scores. Fort Sumter was fired upon; the excitement grew day by day. The time at last arrived when action could no longer be postponed. The President called for 75,000 volunteers for three months' service, and at that time many thought that this small number of men could suppress the rebellion in that brief time.

There was a Regiment of Militia in Vermont and their services were promptly tendered. One of the companies called the Union Guards was located in Middlebury. The college boys were not members, but Lieutenant Rose, and many others of the young men of the village were well known to us. Their departure caused great enthusiasm and the remainder of that college year was full of military activity; war meetings were frequently held, where war speeches were ardent and war songs were enthusiastically received. A company was organized among students comprising nearly every member of the student body, which procured uniforms and arms and assumed the name Middlebury College Guards. Professor Henry M. Seely was its Captain and the other officers were chosen from the different classes. In a short time considerable proficiency in drill was acquired. Meanwhile, the struggle in the South showed no signs of abatement and volunteers were called for to serve for three years, or during the war. From time to time

news was received of the enlistment of those
who had graduated in former years. Some of
the under-graduates left their books and passed
from the college to the camps. The time was
not apt for studious pursuits; bulletins were
more closely scanned than lexicons. The
question, to act or not to act, was presented as
a matter of personal duty. The upper classes
kept substantially intact until their graduation,
after which many of their members sought
the field. Many in the lower classes left
college for the army, usually enlisting from
their homes in different States; a few of these
returned to complete their studies when the
war was over, but most of them disappeared
instantly and forever from the college records.
After the termination of the war in 1865,
several students passed through the college
course who had served their country in the
ranks during the years usually given to the
preparatory school.

It is at this time almost impossible to
prepare a complete roster of Middlebury
College in the war. The general catalogue
fails to state the military service of many
graduates, and of course does not give the
names of those who left College for the army
before graduation.

The following list, including both alumni
and those who did not graduate, is submitted
with the knowledge that it is incomplete, but
its perusal will recall the names of many
whose military service entitles them to the
honor and esteem of all who love their Alma
Mater.

CLASS.

1833—MARK SKINNER, a distinguished jurist in
    Chicago, whose services in connec-
    tion with the Sanitary Commission
    occasioned his election, after the
    conclusion of the war, as an honorary
    member of the Military Order of the
    Loyal Legion of the United States.

1835—NORMAN NELSON WOOD, Chaplain of an
    Illinois regiment.

1836—JOHN BLAKE, Chaplain in the U. S. Navy.

1838—FRANKLIN WHITE OLMSTED, Hospital
    Chaplain.

1840—HENRY NORMAN HUDSON, Chaplain of a
    New York regiment.
        ALEXANDER MILLER, Chaplain of Eighth
    Ohio.
        GEORGE PAGE, Examining Surgeon.

1842—CHARLES LINNAEUS ALLEN, Examining
    Surgeon ; Surgeon of Volunteers ;
    Medical Purveyor, Department of the
    South.

1845—CLAUDIUS BUCHANAN SMITH, Chaplain, U. S. Army.

1847—ASA ELMER EVEREST, U. S. Christian Commission; Chaplain, 118th U. S. C. T.

WARREN WEAVER WINCHESTER, Hospital Chaplain.

1848—DAVIS JOHN RICH, Captain and Asst. Adj.-General, N. Y. Volunteers.

1849—SEWALL SARGEANT, Lieutenant, Captain, Major, 25th N. Y. Volunteer Engineers.

1850—SIMEON SYLVESTER WILLARD, Captain, 98th New York.

1852—JOHN HOWE, 1st Lieutenant, 2d Vermont.

LUCRETIUS DEWEY ROSS, Assistant Surgeon, 14th Vermont; Hospital Surgeon.

1853—BERNICE DAVISON AMES, Secretary Christian Commission.

WILLIAM KEYES, three years' service.

EDWARD PAYSON STONE, Chaplain, Sixth Vermont.

WILLIAM WIRT WALKER, Private, 12th Vermont.

1855—MARTIN LUTHER MEAD, Act'g Asst. Surgeon, 4th Michigan Infantry.

1856—SOLOMON THEOPHILUS ALLEN, Captain, Fourteenth Vermont Volunteers.

GEORGE DANIEL DAVENPORT, Private, Fifth Vermont; Sergeant; First Lieutenant; Captain; killed at the Battle of the Wilderness.

GARDNER WINSLOW GIBSON, First Lieutenant, 17th Vermont Volunteers; mortally wounded at Cold Harbor; died June 14, 1864.

1857—WALTER CHIPMAN DUNTON, Captain, 14th Vermont.

HENRY BENJAMIN FURNESS, Sergeant, 24th Wisconsin Volunteers.

HENRY MARTYN PORTER, Captain; Major; Lieutenant-Colonel; and Colonel, Seventh Vermont; Provost Marshal of New Orleans.

CHARLES WILLIAM SEATON, First Lieutenant; Captain U. S. Sharpshooters; wounded at Malvern Hill.

HORACE HOLMES THOMAS, Captain; Assistant Adjutant-General; Quartermaster-General of Tennessee.

1858—NATHANIEL MERRILL AMBROSE—Private; Sergeant; Major, 30th Maryland Volunteers.

SAMUEL EMMONS BURNHAM, Second Lieutenant; First Lieutenant; Captain, Fifth Vermont Volunteers.

CHARLES SHEPHERD COLBURN, Paymaster's Clerk.

ELIAS DEWEY, Private and Sergeant, 20th Wisconsin.

EPHRAIM T. KELLOGG, Captain, 14th Vermont Volunteers.

JOHN EDWARD PARKER, Corporal and Sergeant, Sixth Vermont.

GEORGE ARDEN ROCKWOOD, Christian Commission; Chaplain, Eighth U. S. C. T.

ALBERT WILSON TRAIN, Served in 159th Ohio Volunteers.

STEPHEN AMBROSE WALKER, Paymaster, U. S. Volunteers.

JAMES MEACH WARNER, A. M., Second Lieutenant, U. S. A.; Colonel 11th Vermont; Brigadier-General, U. S. Volunteers.

1859—MILES POWELL SQUIRE CADWELL, Captain, 22d New York Vol.; killed at the Battle of Bull Run, Aug. 30, 1862.

1860—JOHN QUINCY DICKINSON, Second Lieutenant; First Lieutenant; Quartermaster; Captain of Seventh Vermont; Assistant Commissioner of Freedman's Bureau in Florida; Clerk of Circuit Court; assassinated in 1871.

CHARLES PARMENTER, Representative recruit for Senator J. S. Morrill in 6th Vermont Volunteers; killed at Cedar Creek, Oct. 19, 1864.

GEORGE RICHARDSON, Commissary Sergeant, 14th Vermont Vol.

ELIJAH B. SHERMAN, Second Lieutenant, Ninth Vermont; taken prisoner at Harper's Ferry.

HENRY HOBART VAIL, Sergeant, 121st Ohio Volunteers.

1861—CHARLES EMMET ABELL, Sergeant, 5th Vt. Volunteers; Captain, 14th Vermont Volunteers.

WILLIAM HARVEY BUTTON, Private, 12th Vermont.

SYLVESTER BARRON PARTRIDGE, Private; Second Lieutenant; First Lieutenant, 92d New York; First Lieutenant Signal Corps; Chief Signal Officer, 25th Army Corps.

ERASTUS HIBBARD PHELPS, Paymaster's Clerk.

LINUS ELIAS SHERMAN, First Lieutenant; Captain, Ninth Vermont; taken prisoner at Harper's Ferry.

JAMES BUCHANAN SMITH, First Lieutenant, 25th Massachusetts; Lieutenant Colonel, 36th Massachusetts.

1862—FERNANDO CORTES BEAMAN, Second Lieutenant; First Lieutenant; Captain, 98th New York.

HUGH CRAWFORD CAMPBELL, Private; Corporal; Sergeant, Sixth Vermont.

JOHN ROLLIN CONVERSE, Private; Second Lieutenant, 14th Vermont; Second Lieutenant, 17th Vermont; killed at Petersburgh.

HENRY AUGUSTUS EATON, Private; Captain, 16th Vermont; wounded at Gettysburg; Captain; Major; Lieutenant Colonel, 17th Vermont; killed at Petersburgh.

JOHN ASHLEY FITCH, Sergeant, 12th Vermont.

ELI HOLBROOK GALE, Assistant Surgeon, 186th Pennsylvania.

EDWARD HARMON HOBBS, First Lieutenant; Adjutant, 98th New York; Assistant Adjutant-General, Second Brigade, Casey's Division.

LYMAN ENOS KNAPP, Captain, 16th Vermont; wounded; Captain; Major; Lieutenant Colonel, 17th Vermont.

EDWARD HENRY PETTENGILL, Private, 16th Vermont Volunteers.

DAVID KENDALL SIMONS, Served in Third Tennessee Volunteers.

CHARLES CARROLL SMITH, Private, 14th Vermont Volunteers.

ALDACE FREEMAN WALKER, First Lieutenant; Captain; Major; Lieutenant Colonel, 11th Vermont; Commander Illinois Commandery of Loyal Legion.

1863—DEXTER E. BOYDEN, Private, First Vermont Volunteers; Sergeant, Sixth Vermont Volunteers.

WILLIAM D. BRENNAN, First Lieutenant; Captain; Major, 142d New York.

FRANK G. BUTTERFIELD, A. M., Second Lieutenant; First Lieutenant; Captain, Sixth Vermont.

HENRY M. COBURN, Private, 14th Connecticut Volunteers.

ALBERT ABIJAH CRANE, Sergeant; Second Lieutenant; First Lieutenant, Sixth Vermont Volunteers; killed at the Wilderness, May 5, 1864.

HENRY HERBERT, First Lieutenant, Second U. S. Sharpshooters.

DANIEL HOLMES, Sergeant, 14th Vermont Volunteers.

HARRISON PRINDLE, Adjutant, 14th Vermont Volunteers.

WILLIAM HENRY PROCTOR, Sergeant,
Second U. S. Sharpshooters; Trans-
ferred to the Veteran Reserve Corps;
Second Lieutanant, 24th U. S. Colored
Troops.

ALBERT R. SABIN, Captain, Ninth Vermont; taken prisoner at Harper's
Ferry.

RICHARD STANLEY TUTHILL, First Lieutenant De Golyer's Black Horse Bat-
tery; Michigan Light Artillery; Commander Illinois Commandery of Loyal
Legion.

1864—GEORGE HENRY BAILEY, Private, Sixth
Vermont Volunteers.

HENRY WALLIS BENNETT, Sergeant, First
Vermont Volunteers; died at Fortress
Monroe, June 26, 1861.

FRANCIS GRAY CLARK, Private; Second
Lieutenant; First Lieutenant, 16th
Vermont.

FRANCIS MARION EDGERTON, Adjutant,
Second Vermont Volunteers.

AMASA OSCAR GATES, Sergeant, 17th
Vermont Volunteers; Transferred to
Veteran Reserve Corps.

LEWIS HUNT HEMENWAY, Private, 12th
Vermont.

THEODORE HERBERT, Served in Volunteer Army.

EVELYN VAN NESS HITCHCOCK, First
Lieutenant; Captain, Seventh Vermont.

CHARLES JAY LEWIS, Captain, 11th Vermont Volunteers.

JOHN ABNER MEAD, Private, 12th Vermont.

HENRY DWIGHT SMITH, Q. M. Sergeant;
Sergeant Major, First Vermont Cavalry.

CYRUS THOMAS, Private; Sergeant; Second Lieutenant, 11th Vermont.

EUGENE RANDOLPH WILBER, Captain,
166th N. Y. Volunteers.

JOHN WILLIAMSON, Second Lieutenant;
First Lieutenant of First Vermont
Cavalry; died of a wound received at
Malvern Hill.

EDWARD NELSON WOOD, Served in Volunteer Navy.

1865—HIRAM TAYLOR FRENCH, Second Lieutenant, 142d N. Y. Vols.

EVERTS BRADFORD KENT, Private, Sixth
Vermont; wounded at the Battle of
the Wilderness.

CHARLES GASTINE NEWTON, Second Lieutenant, Tenth Vermont Volunteers;
killed at Battle of Cold Harbor, June
1, 1864.

CHEMICAL LECTURE ROOM.   THE BUILDING LABORATORY.

RILEY E. WRIGHT, Captain, 15th Vermont Volunteers.

1866—EUGENE JOHN RANSLOW, Served in Volunteer Navy; on board "Brooklyn" at bombardment of Fort Fisher.

1867—NATHAN DAVID YALE, Private, First U. S. Sharpshooters.

1868—EDWIN HALL HIGLEY, Sergeant; Lieutenant; Captain; Major, First Vermont Cavalry; prisoner for nine months.

ELMER ELIJAH PHILLIPS, Private, 14th Vermont.

OSCAR DELIEU SCOTT, Private, 17th Vermont; severely wounded.

1869—HORACE FAY WHITE, Private, 14th Vermont.

1870—EUGENE FRANKLIN WRIGHT, Private, Second Vermont.

1871—GIDEON E. CLARK, Private, 11th New York Cavalry; Second Lieutenant and First Lieutenant, U. S. C. T.

HIRAM SMITH JR., Private, 11th Vermont; lost arm and leg; Commander G. A. R., Department of Missouri.

1872—CHARLES EDWARD HALE, Private, 14th Vermont Volunteers.

EDWIN MILES SHERMAN, Sergeant, 11th Vermont Volunteers.

1874—BRADFORD POLK SPARROW, Private, Fourth Vermont Volunteers; taken prisoner.

AUSTIN ORANGE SPOOR, Private, 11th Vermont; in Andersonville Prison.

The following received honorary degrees from Middlebury College, although not graduates:

WILLARD A. CHILD, A. M., Assistant Surgeon, First Vermont; Assistant Surgeon, Fourth Vermont; Surgeon, Tenth Vermont.

JOEL HAYWARD LUCIA, A. M., Private; Sergeant; First Lieutenant, 17th Vermont; wounded at Wilderness.

SAMUEL B. PETTENGILL, A. M., Private, Troop B, Seventh Squadron Rhode Island Cavalry, "College Cavaliers."

EBENEZER J. ORMSBEE, A. M., Second Lieutenant; Captain, First Vermont.

[Errors and omissions there must necessarily be in a list like the preceding, and it is very desirable that such be corrected and amended. Any information bearing on the subject will be gladly received, if sent to the Librarian.]

RELIGIOUS LIFE IN MIDDLE-
BURY.

Coming into existence in one of the Father's pleasant places and cherished by wise and sympathetic friends who relied upon God for help in its support, Middlebury College has ever had "hope and confiding trust in God as its endowments." Even during its first year, there was a revival in the town which affected the college, as the religious life of the college and the community were closely connected.

But this life must have a definite form, so, in 1804, the Philadelphian Society was organized. Its object was "the cultivation of the moral faculties and the religious improvement of its members." Only those students who were members of churches were admitted, and these upon examination. Meetings were held every Friday evening, led by a member or one of the faculty. Once a year a literary contest was held between the strongest men of the Philadelphian and the Philomathesian societies and on the evening of Baccalaureate Sunday a speaker from abroad addressed the society at the regular church service.

A small library of religious and missionary literature was accumulated, numbering, in 1864, 1,135 volumes. This was located in the front of what is now the "English Room" in Painter Hall. The room adjoining was occupied by the Librarian, who held it as a recompense for his services and had access to the library at all times, while the other students drew books only on Wednesdays. The offices of Librarian, President and Secretary were considered honors and were accepted by men chosen from the Senior class.

Closely linked to the Philadelphian Society and often emanating from it are the revivals of which there were ten before 1840, occurring at such intervals that only one class passed through college without coming under such an influence. Some of these continued two or three years, notably the one of 1805. The revivals were "simple, earnest, unostentatious, heart-humbling, and life-reforming." At one time Saturdays were set aside as days of fasting and prayer, and at another, though recitations were not omitted, they were "quiet, solemn, and frequently short, no questions being asked if any one was not prepared to recite." With every new class came a new burden of prayer. And it is because of this feeling of responsibility that Middlebury has "seen more revivals than any other college."

Besides the weekly meetings of the Philadelphians, conference and prayer-meetings were held for a time on Saturday evenings, to which *all* students were invited. Once a week religious instruction was given by some member of the Faculty and this is still continued in the Bible classes in the different Sunday Schools. In regard to other religious exercises, the following selections from the regulation book are of interest:

"The President, or in his absence, one of the Professors or Tutors, shall pray every morning and evening in the chapel, and read a chapter or some suitable portion of Scripture, unless a sermon or some other theological discourse shall be delivered, and the punctual attendance of every student is required."

"Every student shall be obliged to be present at every exercise of public worship on every Lord's day, and on days of public fasting and thanksgiving. No reason of a student's absence from public worship shall be received as sufficient, unless, (when practicable) previously made known to the President, or a Professor, or a Tutor."

As time passed, these rules were gradually disregarded and were replaced a few years ago by some less stringent.

Some time before this it is recorded that the Philadelphian Society held meetings only monthly and in 1876 it existed only in name. In 1878, however, it was reorganized, a new constitution adopted and meetings held regularly until January, 1882, when, through the influence of delegates sent to a convention of Young Men's Christian Associations, it was changed into such an association, adopting the national constitution. It now holds meetings Tuesday evenings, sends delegates to the Northfield and other conferences and obtains the speaker for the evening of Baccalaureate Sunday.

In 1894, the young women, also, formed an association, adopting the national constitution of the Y. W. C. A. They hold meetings Wednesday afternoons in the room which they, with the aid of the Faculty and the Y. M. C. A., have recently fitted up. Every two weeks a class in Bible study follows the regular meeting and in some years one in mission study alternates with this.

Besides work in the college, students have frequently gone into the adjoining districts to hold meetings Sunday afternoons. In 1878, two of the young men held very successful meetings in the jail on Wednesdays, Saturdays and Sundays. One of the young women, sometimes aided by others, established a

Junior **Endeavor Society in town and later** one in a **neighboring village. Several of the** young men **act as supplies in the churches in** the adjoining towns. In fact, **of the students** graduating before 1890, fully **one-third have** pursued the study of theology.

Truly, Middlebury is **a** good training place **for** Christian workers and she ever will be, so **long as she** keeps in mind that "cardinal **doctrine of the** college, that all man's aims, **his disciplined** powers, his acquisitions and all **his cultivated energies** should be consecrated to the good of man and the glory **of God."**

GREEK LETTER SOCIETIES.

IN ORDER OF FOUNDING.

FRATERNITIES.

CHI PSI, founded at Union College, 1841.
   MU CHAPTER established in 1843.

DELTA KAPPA EPSILON, founded at Yale, 1844.
   ALPHA ALPHA CHAPTER established in 1852.

DELTA UPSILON, founded at Williams College, 1834.
   MIDDLEBURY CHAPTER, established in 1856.

PHI BETA KAPPA (honorary), founded at William and Mary College, 1776.
   BETA OF VERMONT CHAPTER established in 1868.

LADIES' SOCIETIES.

ALPHA ZETA of ALPHA CHI (local), founded in 1889.

PI BETA PHI, founded at Monmouth, 1867.
   VERMONT ALPHA established in 1893.

BIRTH-PLACE OF HON. E. J. PHELPS, '40.

THE ADDISON HOUSE.

THE OLD PHRONTISTERION.

THE OLD SOCIETIES.

IN every college there are formed various societies, and it is by these, quite as much as by anything else, that one may form a just estimate of the real character of the students. For these associations are for the most part formed spontaneously, and thus through them the students give expression to their real desires in coming to college. When judged by this standard, the record of our fathers in matters collegiate is recognized as indeed a creditable one. As we recall the various societies of former college days we see how zealously the men of those times strove after wisdom and culture.

The first society formed in Middlebury was the Philomathesian. The exact date of its founding cannot be ascertained, but the College Library contains, among its archives, "The first Judicial book of the Philomathesian Society," dating from October 1, 1802; and the Incorporation of the Society, by act of Legislature, dates from 1822. This society was formed "for the general improvement of the students," and for nearly three-quarters of a century fulfilled its purpose well. Its officers were the usual ones of a literary society. The unique feature of its inner workings was its Judicial Committee. The duties of this committee, which was made up of three members, one from each of the three upper classes, were in part something like this: The secretary having reported, after each meeting, the names of members who had been remiss in the duties laid upon them by the society, it was then the part of the Judicial Committee to judge the validity of the excuses presented. The following extracts will make clear the method of procedure:

To the Judicial Com.:

Gentlemen—On the evening of the 24th of October, (1804), the following members were absent from the Philo. Soc., (viz.): Brs. Bingham, S. P. Blodget, Gray, Harris, Larned, Lawton, Towne Wright, C. Cook, Clark, Berge, Eddy, Hulburt, Akins, G. D. Chipman, R. Hall, Shaw and J. Y. Vale. Attest,

R. C. MALLARY, Scribe.

The Jud. Com. exonerate the above-named absentees except S. P. Blodget, whom we fine six cents.

JOEL DAVIS, } Jud.
WM. SLADE, } Com.

But it appears from this extract of thirty-four years later that evils increased in number with time:

July 18, 1838.

Gent. of Judicial :

There were absent from your last meeting, Douglas 2nd, Harran, Hudson 1st, Kent, Lathrop, McLean, Ranney, Reynolds, Wright, Beckwith 2d, Foster, Hudson 2nd, Miller 1st, Miller 2nd, Sykes, Wainwright and Cook. Tardy—Bingham, Hamilton, Foot. Egressed —Beckwith 1st, Chandler, Cheny, King. Kent and Cook failed to perform.

A. W. DYAR, Secretary.

July 24, 1838.

Mr. Pres. and Gent. Soc. :

Your Committee have fined Douglas 2d, Harran, Kent, Lathrop, Hudson 2d, 12½ cents each for Absence, & Bingham, Foote, 6¼ for tardiness, Beckwith 1st, Cheny, 6¼ for Egression, & Kent and Cook 25 for failures.

"Gent." Jud. Com. { HAMILTON, CHANDLER, WEEKS.

But back in those early days, when we are wont to suppose that every student was just what he should be in the way of devotion to study and much more,—even then all could not have been perfect, it seems, for in the records of 1803 we find this report :

The Jud. Com. in the case of———— ————, which was referred to them by the Society Report: that the said ——— having been degraded from his class, on account of his not having attended to his studies, as a student ought; having been admonished by the President of College; having had a specified time given him, in which he might, by attention to his studies, have regained his former standing; and having still neglected to attend to the exercises of College, has, in our opinion, become a "nuisance" to the College, and a "disgrace" to the society, and ought to be expelled from it.

M. COOK, TH. D. HUGGINS, A. BINGHAM, } Jud. Com.

Although the ideals of this Society were so high, we find passages that indicate at once the fact that human nature is ever the same, while they show also the varied duties of this Judicial Committee and its fidelity in their discharge, as will appear in the following extract from the records of the Committee:

Middy. College, Vt.

2d July, 1838.

ART. 2D. *Resolved,* That your Judicial fine every negligent, wilful, obstreperous and audacious member of your Society; and that said Com. require the secretary to report every delinquent, in all his wayward and disrespectful Conduct; Let favoritism with its attributes be unknown.

ART 3D. *Resolved*, That Your Committee fine all, both Friends and Foes: the latter for past favors, conferred through Official Dignity such as the like, H., C., and Ware fined .25 Cents each for Absence, &c.: the former that they may not become Enemies to themselves and their Friends. The Man who will not step up to the rack and take debate, Composition and mount Pegasus, when it falls to his lot, is, in the Opinion of Your Committee truly an object of severe, sarcastic and unmitigated Censure; and will hereafter be regarded "not only indiscrete and immoral, but highly reprehensible," and will be reproved not by way of reprimand but by "fine if You please, Sir."

Resolved, by Your Committee

ART. 4TH. That an Excuse of this sort, "was necessarily absent," will not answer our purpose, as Jud., but You must go into the minutia in detail. Tell Your business, where you went, whom You saw, how long You staid and the person who offered to see you home or whom You accompanied to the "Gate." The above requirement may appear somewhat arbitrary, at the first view, but not so when sagely considered. Mutual improvement is the ostensible and real object of the Phi. Society: therefore every Member is bound to contribute according to his ability, either by attending the Meetings and participating in its Doings or by relating the history of his abscence; all for mutual improvement.

ART. 5TH. *Resolved*, &c., That Your Com. are not disposed to exercise their official functions and Duties with undue rigor and severity, but being, in our opinion, generous, kind, affectionate, and disbelievers in the "Divine Right of Kings," are disposed to regard the rights of all and preform their Duties with a becoming dignity to the society.

ART. 6TH. *Resolved*, &c., That the fines imposed since last report are hereby remitted, and that each member of said Society is now restored to public favor: and is called upon to maintain the Dignity and Honor of the Society, by an attendance and strict regard to the rules of Propriety. Better be in Texas than to play the fool or to consecrate too much time to the improvement of Your social powers: even if it be spent in the company of the most refined and elevated portion of Community. Reading, thinking, and writing are important for the purpose of developing, aug-

menting and perfecting the intellectual Man:
Neglect the above and Cultivate loquacity, and
soon you will exhibit instead of Mind, the
reckless passions, Curses of Yourselves and
Mankind.

Jud. Com.   { HAMILTON,
             { CHANDLER,
             { WEEKS.

The Philomathesian had a library of about
2400 volumes, especially rich in periodical literature. The privileges of the library were
accorded all members of the Society, to whom
it was open twice a week. Literary meetings
were held weekly, on Wednesdays, at which
compositions and poems were read and questions discussed by members previously appointed. Topics on the slavery question and on
extension of territory were numerous, and
besides were such as these: "Is conscience an
innate principle?" "Do meteoric stones origi-
nate within the atmosphere of the earth?"
"Ought our laws to allow the dissection of the
bodies of friendless strangers?" There were
two occasions yearly when the Philomathesian
held public meetings, and both were very de-
lightful features of college life. At the close
of the Fall term was given the annual Exhibition, consisting of essays, orations, music,
declamations, and a debate by members of the
Senior class. At Commencement time the
Society lured hither some well-known orator
to deliver an address, on which occasion
the President appeared on the stage as the
presiding officer.

For some years the Society was divided into
two divisions, because its membership was so
large, but later these divisions were again
united when the numbers dwindled. And after
the Greek-letter Societies became established,
interest in the Philomathesian became less and
less, until it equaled zero. So the last trace
of the Philomathesian disappeared with the
annual Exhibition in the fall of '67, and
with the Commencement anniversary in the
summer of '68, when Ralph Waldo Emerson
delivered the address.

The next society formed was the Philadelphian, the great religious society of the College, an account of which is given elsewhere.

The Middlebury College Charitable Society
was established in August of 1813, not among
the students, but among "a number of gentlemen in this vicinity." Members of this Society,
however, were not strictly "of this vicinity"
only, but residents of New Hampshire, Massachusetts and Connecticut are also found on the
roll of membership, on which are seen such
names as these: Pres. Davis, Gamaliel Painter,

BELDEN'S FALLS.

IN THE VILLAGE.
CONGREGATIONAL CHURCH IN BACKGROUND.

LAKE DUNMORE.

Samuel Swift, Prof. Hall, John Hough, Thomas Merrill, Bancroft Fowler, Chauncey Langdon, and Joel Linsley. The object of this society was to help young men "of promising talents and unquestioned piety, who were prevented, by pressing poverty, from qualifying themselves to be ministers of the gospel, . . . in obtaining a liberal education." Up to 1817 the Society had given help to sixteen needy students. Up to 1819 it had received in money $3,606.85, but ceased to collect funds about the time of the establishment of the Northwestern Branch of the American Education Society, in 1820, though for some time it continued to extend aid to some of the students at their graduation.

Besides numerous other gifts, the Society received $442.57, in notes, from the Evangelical Society, which had been organized at Pawlet in March, 1804, and which was the first education society established in this country. But the Charitable Society, however gladly it received gifts of money, was also grateful for clothing to distribute among needy students; in fact, an old record of the Society states that "no species of clothing manufactured by either sex, would be unacceptable."

On the Tuesday preceding each Commencement, the Society held a meeting at the Court House, at which an address was delivered and the officers were elected for the ensuing year.

The year 1813 was one fruitful in Societies, for then the Beneficent Society also was formed for the purpose "of providing indigent students with books." Among the names of members of this society may be noticed the following : L. L. Tilden, Thomas Sawyer, L. Miner, James Meacham, Truman Post, P. Battell, Joseph Battell, Asa Hemenway, Francis C. Seymour, Daniel Howard, and J. S. Storrs.

The Beneficent Society had a collection of 850 volumes, which were loaned free of charge to the recipients of its favor and to its members. About 1835 nearly three-fourths of the students were supplied with books from this library.

Through the influence of Professor R. B. Patton (Professor of Greek and Latin from 1818 to 1825), the Philological Society was formed in 1823, the Constitution being adopted on March fifteenth. According to the records of the Society, "several members of Middlebury College assembled for the purpose of forming themselves into a society whose object is to facilitate their progress in Philological researches." Both students' and professors' names appear on the roll of membership. The

Philological had a library of 800 volumes, which the records say was at the service of all members who had paid their fines. Apparently meetings were held when the Society voted, rather than at any regular times, and were usually devoted to literary exercises. The " Society voted that two from each class in catelogical order, exhibit an exercise at each meeting," and accordingly there are programs recorded similar to this: "Dissertation was read by Professor Hough, meeting the objection against the study of the Classics, that it is a relick of the dark ages; also a translation of three odes of Horace."

This Society, in varying degrees of vitality, lived at least until the latter part of the year 1836.

ATHLETICS, PAST AND PRESENT.

IN reviewing the history of our College, we must conclude that the early sports and games bore very small resemblance to modern athletics. Indeed, we almost doubt whether students of the first quarter of a century had any athletic exercise except what they could get from wood-sawing or something equally active. The first reference we find to any kind of systematic exercises is in the *Quarterly Review* of 1831, in which Pres. Bates writes that a Mechanics' Hall had been fitted up for the students, so that they might get necessary physical training. Mechanics' Hall suggests something totally different from the athletics of to-day, and the alumni who were students at that time tell us that the name was a perfectly proper one—that the Hall was simply a workshop, where the student could spend his leisure hours in making useful and salable articles. This Hall was what is now known as the Chester Ross house, which stands near the present Boarding Hall. It was established in 1830 and was in successful operation for several years.

The exercise, however, we must not imagine to be all of such a serious and practical nature. It seems that there was a kind of base-ball played, in which sides were chosen, as now. The rules governing the game were somewhat different from those of base-ball as we know it, though having a few points of resemblance. If the batter missed the ball three times in succession, or if he "ticked " it, and it was caught, he was "out." If he made a "hit," he ran the bases, as now, but if hit between the bases by a thrown ball, he was also "out." There was also in vogue about this time, another game of ball, known as wicket ball. The ball used was about six inches in diameter and was bowled along the ground at a wicket, much as in the present game of cricket.

These games, however, were short-lived, and for a time the fall hunt was the most important athletic event of the year, if it could be classed properly as athletics. This is described in the following article.

Gradually these old-time sports died out and athletics began to assume a modern guise, and but few relics are left to remind us of the athletics of former days, except the modified game of base-ball. In place of the carpenter shop of the thirties and forties, Middlebury students now obtain their exercise in the College gymnasium, working under a competent instructor. Of course base-ball and foot-ball are the leading games, and we have good records in both, although a small college and not able to attract the greatest ball players.

A "cage" would aid greatly in the training of our base-ball men and would increase our reputation in the playing of the national game.

Each of the fraternities owns a tennis court and interest in this branch of athletics is being aroused. Plans are on foot for a Tennis Tournament, and, at no distant day, it is hoped that such a contest can be arranged.

The last Field Day was held in June, 1892, but arrangements have already been made for a revival of the College Meet, on June 4 of this term. The faculty have subscribed money to make a quarter-mile cinder track, and this, with our new grand stand, gives us a splendid equipment for track events. The faculty have also provided prizes for the individual events, and a cup for the class making the best showing. Records are sure to go under, and this Field Day marks a time of great importance in the history of Middlebury Athletics.

On the same day will be held the contests of the Middlebury College Interscholastic meet, in which the schools of this section are represented. Great interest is manifested in these events, and there is no doubt that the Meet will prove the supreme athletic event of the year.

To mention the Cane-rush is to call up a host of recollections of desperate yet friendly struggles. The cane-rush is an old institution, but it is just as popular now as ever. For the two lower classes to test their physical prow-

ess in the cane-rush has come to be an accepted
custom and a healthy one. No bones are
broken, nothing broken but the pride of one
of the two classes.

When we compare our advantages for physical training with those of the early days, we
readily appreciate the progress which has been
made. Middlebury realizes that a sound mind
has its only fitting place in a sound body, and
furnishes the means for the acquirement of
both.

THE COLLEGE HUNT.

DURING Pres. Kitchel's Administration
the "Sugar day" was discontinued and
"College Hunt" instituted. The "modus
operandi" was as follows: The students
met in the chapel and elected two captains
who chose the students, after having tossed
a penny for first choice. Then the captains
arranged a scale of points for the different
kinds of game. This scale generally began
with the bear and ended with the chipmunk,
but by special request anything that flies,
runs or swims, was included. One year,
fish were counted, and two of the boys
secured a count of over three thousand on
minnows. At another time potato bugs
were counted and one side brought in
several quarts of the beetles.

It seemed to be generally understood that
each man would get all the help he could
and generally some rather "old" game was
brought in. The hunt usually began some
time Friday and closed at 6 P. M. on Saturday. The count then took place and the
victorious side was announced. After
this, those who had previously voted for it,
repaired to the hotel and partook of a feast
at the expense of the vanquished side.

The custom prevailed for a few years,
perhaps four or five, and ended tragically,
when a member of the class of '76 acci-
dentally shot himself in the leg.

As viewed from a distance of twenty-one
years, the only merit of "College Hunt"
was an opportunity for a few to make up
back work and the many to acquire a famous
appetite for supper, while its great demerit
was the useless slaughter of small animals
like red squirrels, chipmunks and small
birds, not strictly game.

EARLY HISTORY OF THE TOWN OF MIDDLEBURY.

THE history of Middlebury begins at the same time as the histories of the two neighboring towns of New Haven and Salisbury. These three towns were surveyed early in 1760, by John Evarts, Esq., who was agent for a company of men residing at Salisbury, Conn. After finishing the survey, Evarts applied to Benning Wentworth, Governor of New Hampshire, for charters, in the name of this company. The charters were granted on the second and third of November, 1761. The southern town was named Salisbury from the place in Connecticut where the proprietors sided; the northern was named New Haven from the well-known city in the same State; the middle one was then appropriately called Middlebury.

The first settler in the town was John Chipman, who came into the wilderness in 1766, five years after it had been chartered by the New Hampshire Governor. He cleared about eight acres of land on the north bank of Middlebury river, but being discouraged with the prospects, went to Connecticut and did not return until 1773. By this time, however, another pioneer had arrived. His name was Benjamin Smalley. He brought his family with him, and was the first to construct a dwelling house in the town limits. It was a rude structure. There was no sawmill within many miles, and the house was necessarily built of logs. The roof and the floors were made of bark.

Within a few weeks of Smalley's arrival, John Chipman returned, bringing his family with him. At this time, also, another pioneer came, Gamaliel Painter, a man of rare sense and judgment, destined to be the "father of the town," and one of the greatest benefactors of our college. He was born in New Haven, Connecticut, May 22, 1742, and lived seventy-six years. His name will ever be associated with the history of the institution.

On coming to Middlebury in 1773, he, also, brought his family with him. So Chipman and Painter immediately began the erection of houses similar to the one in which Smalley was then living. During this year three more men with their families came and began clearing up land and building houses. These men were Eleazer Slawson, James Owen, and Samuel Bentley. Thus by the year 1774, Middlebury was becoming quite a settlement. While other towns were being troubled by the con.

flicting claims 'of the New York and New
Hampshire grantees, Middlebury was steadily
growing. New York never made any grants
in Middlebury.

On account of the prospering condition of
affairs at the beginning of this year, the
proprietors, to encourage the erection of a
sawmill, offered to give a lot on which one
might stand to the person who would build it.
This offer was accepted by a new settler, Abisha
Washburn, who constructed a mill on the east
side of the village falls. He sold this mill
later to Chipman and Painter. The first school
house was built the following year, 1775. It
was about twelve feet square, made of small
logs and poles, with a roof of bark. The school
was taught by Miss Eunice Keep, a half sister
of John Chipman

While the settlement was in this growing
condition, the Revolutionary war broke out.
After the defeat of Montgomery at Quebec,
the frontier was constantly exposed to the
marauding expeditions of the British and Indians; so nearly all the inhabitants of that
region were compelled to abandon their hard-
earned homes. At Middlebury all left with
the exception of Daniel Foot and Benjamin
Smalley. They remained until the close of
the year 1776, when a force of Indians ap-
proached, making it necessary for them to
leave for the larger settlements. They returned, however, the following winter and
remained until the spring of 1778.

At the close of the war most of the settlers
returned. They found that nearly all their
buildings had been destroyed. The only ones
which remained standing were three log houses
situated in remote places. It is supposed that
they were not discovered by the pillaging
parties. The sawmill was burned and the settlement left in a very uninviting condition.
Many of the settlers had taken part in the war.
John Chipman retired as a colonel. He was
with Ethan Allen at the taking of Forts Ticon-
deroga and Crown Point, and was in the battles
of Bennington and Saratoga. At one time he
was in command of Fort George. Judge
Painter also took part in the war, visiting the
enemy several times as a spy, to ascertain the
condition and plans of the British. He was
also delegate for the Middlebury settlers at the
convention at Dorset on Sept. 25, 1776; and
again at the convention at Westminster, Jan.
15, 1777, which declared the New Hampshire Grants a free and independent State.

On the return of the settlers, the advantage
of being near the falls seems to have dawned
upon them, and the present village of Middle-

bury was started. The first house to be built
within the limits of the village was erected by
John Johnson, in 1783. It stood on the west
side of the river, near the bank and a short
distance above the falls. He used it as a ferry
house, and his business was to carry passen-
gers across the river. In 1784 Daniel Foot
built a sawmill and gristmill. It was on the
west side of the river, was 30 by 60 feet in
dimensions, and was opened for business in
November, 1785. The mill was a great benefit
to the town. Hitherto they had been obliged to
go to Pittsford for all their grinding, and on
account of poor roads the river had been used
as a means of communication. This took a
great amount of time and labor, so the mill
was a great saving to the inhabitants.

In 1787 Daniel Foot again benefited the town
by constructing a bridge across the river, thus
joining the two towns which the river had sep-
arated. It was seen subsequently that greater
benefits would result to the inhabitants along
the two banks if they were to be in the same
town. So, later, when the population had increased on each bank, the problem of uniting
a portion of the western bank to Middlebury
was brought up. In the early survey the town-
ship had extended from the river towards the
east. After much discussion, by an act of the
Legislature, a strip of territory one mile in
width was taken from the adjacent town of
Cornwall and annexed to Middlebury, March
14, 1796. The first town meeting had been held
on March 29, 1786. The officers chosen were
Moderator, Town Clerk and Constable. No
other officers were chosen until 1788, when the
town was fully organized and represented in
the Assembly.

The first school in the village was kept by
Mrs. Goodrich, wife of William Goodrich,
Esq. It was opened in 1791 in a small school
house opposite her own home. From this time
the village grew rapidly, many able men coming there to live. The town affairs were run
in a very business-like manner. In 1797 the
Addison County Grammar School was chartered and a few years later, in 1800, a few
stores were started in the place. Thus, at the
time the college was founded, in the latter
part of this year, Middlebury was a flourishing
village. It had been made the shire town of
the county, had a population of thirteen hundred, supported a weekly paper called the
Gazette, and had among its inhabitants lawyers,
physicians, merchants, mechanics and artists.
From a wilderness in 1766, by the energy of
those early men it had survived the desolation
and the destruction of the war, and in the brief

space of thirty-four years, was made ready to foster an institution of learning whose influence was to spread abroad over every land. Those old heroes who braved all the elements of danger and hardship and thereby founded the home of our Alma Mater, deserve our deepest interest. Their work was difficult, but it was successfully accomplished. From them the Middlebury man has learned his lessons of industry and perseverance, and to them and to their history he will continue to look, finding there the inspiration and the teaching which will guide him to duty and final success.

SONG.

[*Air, John Brown's Body.*]

I.

COME and join us in a song
    Of good old college days!
Let your voices free and strong
    A sounding chorus raise!
Loyalty and love belong
    To Her we proudly praise,
            Our Alma Mater dear!

Chorus:

Middlebury live forever!
Middlebury live forever!
Middlebury live forever!
    Our Alma Mater dear!

II.

Sophomores and Freshmen, who
    Have battled for the cane,
Will rally 'neath the White and Blue
    As brothers once again!
Upper-classmen gladly too,
    Will join in the refrain,
            Our Alma Mater dear!

Chorus:

III.

Laugh away the fleeting years
    For soon our college days
Will vanish with their joys—and tears,
    Their gay, half-earnest ways!
Still, whatever fate appears,
    Her loyal sons will praise
            Our Alma Mater dear!

Chorus:

IV.

Mix a cup of kindness then,
    Let college spirit flow!
Pledge to Her as college men
    The homage that we owe!
Ring the chorus out again,
    That all the world may know,
            Our Alma Mater dear!

Chorus:

C. W. PRENTISS, '96.

PRES. EZRA BRAINERD.

PROF. W. W. EATON

FACULTY AND OFFICERS.

——o——

EZRA BRAINERD, LL. D. President.

Professor of Mental and Moral Science.

A. B., Middlebury, 1864; A. M., 1867; LL. D. in 1888, from the University of Vermont and Ripon College; first Parkerian Prize; Philosophical Prize; Valedictorian.

Tutor in Middlebury College, 1864-65; graduated from Andover Theological Seminary, 1868; Professor of Rhetoric and English Literature in Middlebury, 1868-80, of Physics and Applied Mathematics, 1880-91; President pro tempore, 1885-86; President, 1886—; Professor of Mental and Moral Science, 1891-.

Member of Board of Commissioners, appointed to revise the school laws of the State of Vermont, 1887; President of the Vermont Botanical Club; non-resident member of New England Botanical Club; and member of American Geological Society.

————

WILLIAM WELLS EATON, A. M.,

Professor of Greek Language and Literature.

A. B., Amherst, 1868; A. M., 1871. Took prizes in Mathematics (2), Greek, Physics, and General excellence; Valedictorian.

Instructor in Academy, Monson, Mass., 1868-69; student in Andover Theological Seminary, 1869-71; Instructor in Phillips Academy, Andover, Mass., 1871-73; student in Classical Philology in Göttingen and Leipsic, Germany, 1873-76; Instructor in Greek in Andover Theological Seminary, 1877-80; engaged in literary work, assisting in the translating of Thayer's New Testament Greek Lexicon, 1880-82; Professor of Greek in Middlebury, 1882-84, of Greek and German, 1884-93; Professor of Greek Language and Literature, 1893-.

————

HENRY MARTYN SEELY, A. M., M. D.

Professor Emeritus of Natural History.

Ph. B., Yale, 1856; M. D., Berkshire Medical School, 1857; A. M., Yale, 1860.

Assistant in Chemistry, Analytical Laboratory, Yale, 1857; Professor of Chemistry, Berkshire Medical School, 1857-61; Professor of Chemistry, Medical Department, University of Vermont, 1860-67; Professor of Chemistry and Natural History, Middlebury, 1861-92; of Natural History, 1892-95; Professor Emeritus of Natural History, 1895-.

At Royal **Mining** School, Freiburg, **Saxony**, 1867; at **University of** Heidelburg, Baden, 1868; Secretary **of Vermont** State Board of Agriculture, 1875-78; **Edited** three volumes of Agricultural Reports; **Member of** American Chemical Society; of Geological Society of **America;** of Biological Society of Washington.

CHARLES BAKER WRIGHT, A. M.

PROFESSOR OF RHETORIC AND ENGLISH LITER-ATURE AND LIBRARIAN.

A. B., Buchtel College, 1880; A. M., 1885. **Johns** Hopkins University, 1882-85; Graduate Scholar of J. H. U., 1884-85; Fellow of J. H. U., 1885; Chair of Rhetoric and English Literature at Middlebury, 1885-.

WALTER E. HOWARD, LL. D.,

PROFESSOR OF HISTORY AND POLITICAL SCIENCE.

A. B., Middlebury, 1871; admitted to bar in Wisconsin, 1873; practiced law in Milwaukee, 1873-76; Principal State Normal School at Castleton, Vt., 1876-78; resigned to accept a similar position in Tennessee; resumed practice of law, in Fair Haven, Vt., in 1881; elected to Senate **of** Vermont in 1882, resigning **to** become United States Consul at Toronto, Ontario, under President Arthur; representative in the Legislature in 1888, being largely instrumental in securing State scholarships for **the** colleges in Vermont: Professor of history and Political Science at Middlebury, 1889-92; United States Consul at Cardiff, **Wales, 1892-3;** resumed professorship **in** Middlebury, **1893-**.

MYRON REED SANFORD, A. M.,

PROFESSOR OF LATIN LANGUAGE AND LITERA-TURE.

A. B., Wesleyan, 1880; A. M., Wesleyan, 1883; Spinney Greek Prize; Olin Rhetorical Prize; Squire Scholarship, and First Honors in Greek.

In charge of Classical Department, Wyoming Seminary, Kingston, Pa., 1880-86; Assistant Professor of Latin and Registrar, Haverford College, 1886-87; Professor of Latin (same), **1887-90;** Professor of Latin and **Dean of College** (same), 1890-93; Professor of Latin, Middlebury College, 1894-.

Göttingen and Rome, summer of 1892; student in Classical Philology in University of Leipsic, 1893-94; studied Archaeology in Rome, 1894.

PROF. HENRY M. SEELY.

PROF. C. B. WRIGHT.

PROF. WALTER E. HOWARD.

WILLIAM WESLEY McGILTON, A. M.,
Professor of Chemistry.

A. B., Wesleyan University, 1881; Commencement Orator; A. M., 1884; Vice-President and Instructor in Science, Fort Edward Collegiate Institute, 1881–91; traveled in Europe, 1882; student in Chemistry and Physics, Leipsic University, Germany, 1891–92; Professor of Chemistry in Middlebury, 1892–.

THEODORE HENCKELS,
Professor of Modern Languages.

B. Sc., University of Ghent, 1881; winner of Belgian Government Fellowship in the École Normale Superieure (Scientific Section), 1881–83; Teacher of Latin, French, Arithmetic and Physics in Charlier Institute, New York, 1883–85; Teacher of German and French in Clinton Liberal Institute and Director of Potter Business College, Fort Plain, N. Y., 1885–87; Master of Modern Languages and of Mechanical and Free-hand Drawing at St. Matthew's Hall, San Mateo, Cal., Feb. to Sept., 1887; Instructor in German at Cornell University, Sept., 1887–91; Post-Graduate Student in the Germanic Languages at Harvard, 1891–92, and Instructor in French at Harvard University and Radcliff College, 1891–94; since 1894 Professor of Modern Languages in Middlebury; Contributor to periodicals and Editor of Modern Language Texts.

ERNEST CALVIN BRYANT, B. S.,
Professor of Mathematics and Physics.

Graduated from Middlebury, 1891; four Waldo Prizes, second Botanical Prize, Salutatorian; graduated from Mass. Institute of Technology, 1893; employed by Canadian Bridge and Iron Co., Montreal, P. Q., 1893–95; Professor of Mathematics and Physics in Middlebury, 1895–.

EDWARD ANGUS BURT, Ph. D.,
Burr Professor of Natural History.

Graduated at State Normal School, Albany, N.Y., in 1881; A. B., *summa cum laude* (Harvard), 1893; A. M. (*ibid*), 1894; Ph. D. (*ibid*), 1895.

At Harvard, was awarded in 1893 a Bowdoin prize for a dissertation on *The Origin of Variations in Organism*; received Highest Final Honors in Natural History at graduation in 1893; awarded a Bowdoin prize for a dissertation on *The Evolution of Sexuality*, in 1894; was Morgan Fellow in botany in 1894–95.

Taught three terms in common schools of New York during course at the Normal School; taught Natural Science and other subjects in Albany Academy, N. Y., 1880–85; Examiner in Natural Science for Regents of Univ. of State of N. Y., 1882–86; Professor of Natural Science in State Normal School, Albany, N. Y., 1885–91; admitted to the Junior Class at Harvard in 1891; Burr Professor in Natural History in Middlebury College, 1895–.

His botanical writings have been published in Science, 1893; Memoirs of Boston Society of Natural History, 1894; Annals of Botany, 1896; Botanical Gazette, 1896.

Is a member of the American Microscopical Society, the Vermont Botanical Club and the Society for Vegetable Morphology and Physiology, and a non-resident member of the New England Botanical Club.

CHARLES EDWARD PRENTISS, A. M., M. D.,

ASSISTANT LIBRARIAN.

A. B., Middlebury, 1864; A. M., 1867; M. D., Georgetown University, 1868; in U. S. Treasury Department, banking business and practice of medicine, Washington, D. C., 1864–82; in business, Middlebury, Vt., 1883–88; in publishing business, New York City, 1888–91; Assistant Librarian, 1896–.

IN A SOCIAL VEIN.

"All Work and no play makes Jack a dull Boy."

MIDDLEBURY students, like other college students, generally manage to have enough of fun mixed in with their work to make them resemble not in the least the above mentioned "Jack." At any rate, we students of the present day find it so, and records of twenty years ago show that the students of "Old Midd." were not then entirely free from social enjoyments. And most probably Middlebury has always, from her start, had more or less to do with the social side of life.

The principal seasons of social events are the fall and spring, though the winter, too, has its share. As soon as college opens in the fall, receptions and parties begin, which keep the poor Freshman in such a whirl of excitement that he is forced to wonder, when, if such things are kept up the whole year round, he will ever find time for the numerous studies for the sake of which he came to college. First comes the joint reception of the Y. M. and Y. W. C. A. to the Freshman class. Following close upon the heels of this come numerous "select" receptions, given by different fraternities, and small private "spreads" given in interest of fraternities. There are boat rides on Otter Creek, picnics to Lake Dunmore, Snake Mountain, or Bread Loaf Inn, and other events of a similar nature.

At the end of the fall term comes Junior Promenade—a dance given by the Junior class for the purpose of making money. Sometimes the purpose is gained ; often times not. Then at the end of the winter term comes Junior Exhibition, which is followed by a dance. Formerly this was called Junior Quarterly and following is an invitation given by the Junior Class in 1808:

JUNIORS' QUARTER BALL.

—:o:—

The Company of..................
is requested at Bell's Assembly Hall, on Wednesday, 6th of April, at 6 o'clock P. M.

H. BELL, Junr., } Managers. { B. EDGERTON,
D. D. DEMING, }   { T. LELAND.

Middlebury, March 20, 1808.

But now, *the* social time of the year is Commencement, whose gaieties last nearly a week. And even in olden times this was the gayest time of the year. Then, everybody from far and near came to Commencement, and preparations were in progress for weeks beforehand for their generous entertainment. Booths and shanties were profusely scattered along the road, whereat good meals could be obtained for small prices. But the war put an end to this custom, and it has never been wholly revived. Now, as then, people gather from far and near, but they are mostly alumni— or alumnæ,—and every undergraduate determines that he too will come back with the rest, to his Alma Mater's Commencement, just as often as his worldly cares will permit.

All work is finished, for the Seniors, two weeks before college closes, and all examinations are over for the rest by Friday night before the Wednesday that the Commencement exercises proper are held. The fun begins Saturday with the "rides" given by the men's fraternities. Each fraternity, with ladies who are so fortunate as to be invited, starts off to spend the day somewhere. The ladies are sometimes kept in ignorance of where, until the last minute, which causes

intense excitement **at times**. They **go by**
train, by carriage, **or both**, sometimes, **to**
Burlington for a ride on Lake Champlain, or
to Lake George, or to Vergennes, and thence
up the Otter Creek and Lake Champlain to
Ausable Chasm, or perhaps to Bread Loaf Inn
to spend the day, always *planning* to get in
before the town clock chimes forth the hour of
twelve, telling that Sunday is at hand. Sunday
exercises would hardly **come** under social
events, so we **pass** to Monday afternoon and
the class **day exercises.** All interested in
these meet on the **campus soon** after dinner
and, up to this time, **this has** always proved
an exceedingly interesting occasion.

On Monday evening for **several** years **it
has been** the custom for the young ladies of
the town and college to return the compliments
paid them by the young gentlemen throughout
the year by giving a dance. Some might not
call this properly a social function of the
college, but if it were not for the college
there would surely be no dance given at that
particular time.

Tuesday is Alumni Day. Exercises are held
in the Congregational Church in the morning,
and at noon is the banquet. After the dinner
the alumni reception is held at the house of
one of the Faculty. On that evening come the
Parker and Merrill prize speaking contests.
After this the fraternities meet in their several
fraternity homes, to rejoice in company with
their alumni members over the victories they
have won, **or should have** won, a few hours
before. These **banquets** often last into **the**
"wee sma' hours" of Wednesday morning.
Later on that same morning comes the alumni
meeting, and **then** the graduating exercises.
Twenty years ago it used to be the fashion to
throw flowers at the speaker. The fellow who
had **the** largest assortment **of** "sisters" or
"flames," or who was moderately or " more
so " handsome used to be plentifully supplied
with bouquets. But this custom has **now**
died out. After the exercises comes **the**
announcing of honors, and then the corporation
dinner, passing which, **we come to** the grand
finale, the Concert and **Ball.**

It might be interesting to turn for a moment
to the first Commencement Ball Middlebury
ever held, **in 1802.** The whole graduating
class consisted **of Mr. Aaron** Petty, and dis-
banded **in** 1803, upon his death. This class
established the custom ever since observed
here, and gave Middlebury's first Commencement Ball in Stowell's Hall, which was built
that year on Weybridge street. The invitation
was as follows:

PROF. MYRON R. SANFORD.

PROF. W. W. McGILTON.

PROF. THEODORE HENCKELS.

COMMENCEMENT BALL.

M._____Attendance
is requested at Mr. Stowell's
Assembly Hall, at 6 o'clock P. M.

A. Petty,   Managers   M. Cook,
W. Chapin, Middlebury College, F. E. Hale,
H. Chipman,   1802.   F. D. Huggins.
Tickets to be left at Door.

Chipman and Chapin were 1803 men, Cook,
Hale and Huggins, 1804.

Now the Senior Class sends out to its
numerous friends invitations for the whole
series of gaieties. All accept who can, for the
Ball at least. By eleven o'clock on Wednesday Eve, all are assembled in the Town Hall,
and the lights are shining "o'er fair women
and brave men;" and then, as the music
quickens with all "its voluptuous swell,"—it
is the old story; you know the rest. But as
the sky begins to grow lighter, showing the
appearance of dawn, and the music of "Home,
Sweet Home," the last waltz, grows fainter,
fainter, and finally dies away, 'tis then that
the newly fledged alumnus has that "lonely,
sad feeling," as he thinks that it is all over
and his undergraduate career is closed.

THE LIBRARY—1800-1897.

I.

WHEN Thomas Clap, away back in
1766, published his "Annals of Yale
College," he told this interesting story of the
founding of that institution: "Ten of the
principal Ministers in the Colony were nomi-
nated to found . . . a College; . . .
which they did . . . in the following Manner, viz: Each Member brought a number of
books and presented them to the Body, and, lay-
ing them on the Table, said these words, or to
this effect: '*I give these Books for the founding
a College in this Colony.*' Then the Trustees,
as a Body, took Possession of them, and
appointed the Rev. Mr. *Russel* of *Branford*
to be the Keeper of the Library, which then
consisted of about forty Volumes in Folio."
These words of the ten ministers have the
right ring; they show a sound conception of
the place of book collections in systems of
higher education. And Carlyle, exactly one
hundred years later, in his Rectorial Address
to the students of Edinburgh University, gave
utterance to the same truth, when he told
what the University had done for him.

It is the purpose of this article to show from the library records that Middlebury not only equals Yale in the matter of library founding, but goes her one better in a rather remarkable way. Yale College and the Yale library came into existence together; the Middlebury College library antedates the college itself by at least six months.

In his historical sketch of the college, written for the *Quarterly Register* in 1837, Professor Fowler states that "the college library was commenced in 1809, by a number of public spirited individuals, who subscribed something like a thousand dollars for the purchase of books." An old blank book in the possession of the library, containing the first catalogue and lists of proprietors and patrons, together with a record of the books they drew, abundantly disproves the statement. The first page bears the inscription, "Middlebury College Library Accounts, April, 1800." On page three is given a list of those "students in the Academy" who drew from the library stores. First on the list stands Harry Chipman, of whom it is recorded, page five, that on Oct. 6, 1800, he paid in advance to the librarian the sum of fifty cents, drawing on the same day his first book, as charged on page sixty-four, the same being the "Son of Ethelwolf." This Harry Chipman appears as a Junior in the first catalogue of the college, Nov. 17, 1801; it must, then, have been at least one year earlier that he figured as a "student in the Academy," which confirms the 1800 date. Proofs differing merely in detail could be multiplied from the volume, but the one given will suffice.

It may, perhaps, appear rather strange to some that a collection of books, known as the Middlebury College Library, should have been in use before the existence of Middlebury College itself. A simple explanation is found in the circumstances that attended the securing of a college charter. The petition of Gamaliel Painter and others for a charter of incorporation was presented to the legislature Oct. 31, 1798, though that charter was not granted till Nov. 1, 1800. That the advanced work of the Addison County Grammar School was in the meantime of a collegiate grade (as curricula then went), is indicated by the fact that Aaron Petty, an academy student, took rank as a Senior in the first college catalogue and graduated in 1802. It is not strange, therefore, that in the spring of 1800 those in charge of the books then owned should have designated the collection as the Middle-

bury College Library; the college had a *de
facto* existence already, and it was doubtless
known by that time that the legislature
which was to convene the coming fall in Middlebury would give it an existence *de jure.*
And so it came about that the library, as a
working institution, has a continuous history
reaching back beyond the charter.   A continuous history is said advisedly, for the first
eighteen books of the library, as originally
numbered in the spring of 1800, are the first
eighteen in the numbering of to-day—the
first American edition of a foreign encyclo-
pedia, published in Philadelphia in 1798.

II.

The library is at present located in the north
division of Painter Hall.   The four floors,
each thirty feet square, are devoted to its use,
together with a commodious reading and
reference room in the middle division adjacent.   To the volumes of the first catalogue
there have been added, in the intervening
years, some 20,000 more, each book accessible
to every library user.   There are no treasures
of special value or importance, though many
of the volumes, through association, are worthy of notice.   Professor William Chauncey
Fowler, who from 1828 to 1838 occupied the
chair of chemistry and natural history, was a
son-in-law of Noah Webster and a co-laborer
in the preparation of the dictionary.   As a
result, the earlier editions of that work have a
pleasant local flavor in their illustrative examples.   A number of interesting volumes bear
the presentation autograph of the great dictionary maker.

The efficiency of the library as a working
center has steadily grown.   As the facilities
for work increase, its use is more and more
required of students by the various instructors.
Constant reference is made in class-room to
books by volume and page.   Works helpful
in the investigation of special subjects are
reserved in shelves upon the first floor.   A
higher grade of scholarship and study has thus
been made possible.

It is hoped that the college will be able to
celebrate its centennial in 1900 by the dedica-
tion of a new library building.   For this the
plans have already been prepared under the
direction of Dr. Henry H. Vail, '60, of New
York; the cut at the end of this article is from
the perspective drawing of the architect.

These plans, if executed, will result in a beautiful structure costing some $50,000, and admirably adapted to making possible the most approved library methods.

THE MUSEUM.

TO Charles Baker Adams, Professor of Chemistry and Natural History in the College from 1838 to 1847, are largely due the objects of interest which go to make up the Museum. A nucleus there probably was around which he arranged his collections when he came to his chair of instruction, but up to this time it has not been possible to make a definite statement in the matter, though a list of twenty-six articles "for the museum of Middlebury College," written in the earliest record-book of the Library, bears some internal evidence of having been put there before 1810.

Professor Adams collected in many fields of science, and got together by gift, purchase, exchange and by his own labor, a grand mass of material for illustrating the branches he taught; especially representing Mineralogy, Geology and Zoology. These he catalogued with perfect system and extreme care. He was eminent as a conchologist, and his collection of shells will remain a memorial of him and his work. Especially to be prized is a collection of shells representing the Mollusca of Vermont.

Professor Adams was also at one time State Geologist of Vermont, and he placed upon the shelves of the Museum a most valuable numbered and labeled suite of the rocks of Vermont, which he had gathered for the college while in his official duties connected with the State survey.

After the resignation of Professor Adams until near the year 1861, there is mostly a gap in the record of additions to the Museum. One notable gift, however, fitting into this time, was that made by Rev. Dr. C. F. Muzzy, class of 1832, missionary to India. Dr. Muzzy

PROF. E. C. BRYANT,

PROF. E. A. BURT.

DR. C. E. PRENTISS.

gathered and sent home rocks and fossils representing the cretaceous formation of the localities he visited, he becoming in the meantime a geologist of note. Among the examples sent is the magnificent sliced ammonite in one of the cases.

Perhaps the most valued single piece contributed to the Museum was obtained by Rev. Dr. W. A. Farnsworth, class of 1848, for a long time a missionary to Cesarea, Turkey; the Nineveh slab, standing at the east end of the room. Excavated from its long resting place, it was sawn into smaller squares for convenience of packing, transported hundreds of miles on camel's back to the sea, thence to our shores by ship. The sawed pieces were cemented and the slab, with its cuneiform inscription and its heroic figure, seems almost as fresh as when it left the chisel of the sculptor, thousands of years ago.

"They builded better than they knew." The old saw gets a new setting. The Assyrian workmen thought they were preparing a slab to grace the temple of their master, and so adorned it with figure and enduring words of praise. But really they were cutting a memorial slab for the Museum of Middlebury College; a stone which shall mark the love of one of her sons who has given his best life to the service of the one true Master.

About 1866, the Cabinet of General Martin Fields of Newfane, Vt., was given to the college. The collection consisted largely of minerals from the eastern part of the State, together with a good number from foreign parts.

A little later, by exchange with Professor Albert Hard, class of 1850, of Knox College, Ill., a prized collection of cretaceous fossils was secured for the Museum.

Still later, from Professor C. W. Hall, class of 1871, of the University of Minnesota, a representative suite of the rocks and fossils of Minnesota has been received.

Near 1876 a purchase of casts and actual examples for illustration of Palæontology was made from the Ward establishment in Rochester, N. Y. These forms have been of much service in the class room.

A collection representing the rocks of the Champlain valley, from the Archean up through the Potsdam, Calciferous, Chazy, Trenton, to the Utica Slate, has been placed in the drawers in the north side of the room for class instruction.

Perhaps the most noted contribution to the natural history of the State, after those of Professor Adams, was the discovery, by several members of the Faculty of the college, in 1880, at Fort Cassin, on a little promontory at the mouth of Otter Creek, a station of Calciferous fossils; a gathering in the rocks, of fossil forms, scarcely less than marvelous.

The place had been made historic in 1814 by the success of Lieutenant Cassin, with a handful of sailors and soldiers, in beating back an attempt of a British force to ascend the river with the purpose of burning Macdonough's fleet, then building at Vergennes. Here, within a small space, on the site of the earthworks, and in the loose stones, built into a protecting wall, were found, besides well known forms, near forty fossil species new to science. These examples, described by Professor Whitfield of the American Museum of New York City, have representatives on the shelves and in the drawers of the Museum.

When, under the administration of President Hamlin, the college library was transferred from the second floor of the chapel building to the north division of Painter Hall, the Museum collections were removed to the vacated rooms, where, in new cases, the display is much more satisfactory. The replacing of the specimens on the shelves was mostly the work of Professor B. F. Koons, now President of the Storrs Agricultural College of Connecticut. From him were received a good number of marine specimens in Zoology of his own gathering, while connected with the U. S. Fish Commission; and an additional gift of like character was made to the college by Professor S. F. Baird of the Smithsonian Institution.

The specimens of birds, with eggs and nests, were largely contributed by Professor F. H. Knowlton of the class of 1884, now with the Smithsonian Institution and the U. S. Geological Survey. Also, a collection of birds and small mammals has been given by Rev. Mr. Bailey, at one time a member of the class of 1864.

The notable casts, copies of Egyptian divinities, the Decree of Canopus, tablets, and so forth, were obtained for the college by the Rev. Dr. Henry M. Ladd of the class of 1872.

The Alaskan objects, illustrative of the common life of the northern Indians, were gifts of Rev. John W. Chapman, class of 1879, of Christ Church Mission, Anvik, Yukon Valley. As objects of this character are passing from use and from existence, displaced by articles from civilized life, their value is enhanced by the passage of time.

The examples of Archæology and Ethnology are mostly unlisted. They have nearly all come in as gifts from the finders. A place three miles or so south of Middlebury seems

THE PRESIDENT'S HOUSE.

A CORNER IN THE MUSEUM.

to have been a favorite fishing and camping ground of the Indians, and in the vicinity many relics abound. In his field, the late James Madison Piper ploughed up a fine stone pestle, and this he gave to the College Museum, where it finds its place on the shelves with objects of like character.

The complete collection of the Vascular Cryptogams and the flowering plants of the State of Vermont was prepared and put into the Museum as a gift by President Brainerd.

Many gifts unmentioned here, and of great value, have been presented by the friends of the college. Most of these are properly accredited to the donor. It is the purpose to give due credit to every person who has had a kind thought toward the college, and has expressed that thought by a gift. It is to be regretted that at present the names of some who have made valued presents to the Museum are unknown, but it is hoped that, on further search and inquiry, these names will be restored to the labels that mark the objects. Until this is done, the visitor to the Museum will perhaps kindly bear in mind and read with the description the uninscribed legend, "Thanks to the unnamed donor."

The additions to the Museum since 1861 have been mostly made under the supervision of Professor Henry M. Seely. By work in the field, by solicitation and by exchanges, the examples in mineralogy and geology coming in since that year have been largely obtained by him.

A WORD IN PARTING.

THE editors wish to express their gratitude to all those who have in any way helped them in their attempt to carry out the enterprise they had in mind. Especial thanks are due to Col. Aldace F. Walker of the class of '62, for his kindness in contributing the article on "Middlebury College in the War," to Prof. Henry M. Seely, for the facts in regard to the Museum, and to Prof. Wright for the story of the Library. To Prof. Boyce we are indebted for the facts concerning the College Hunt, and to Rev. E. J. Ranslow, '66, for additional facts on the subject of "Middlebury College in the War." We wish to express our thanks to Rev. Dr. J. E. Rankin, '48, and Mr. C. W. Prentiss '96, for contributions of verse, and to D. P. Hurlburt, '99, and T. F. Tangney, 1900, for assistance in designing and sketching. Prof. Wright and Dr. Prentiss have helped us very materially by assistance in editing, verifying facts, and reading proof, and we wish to express our appreciation of their kindness. Without the financial backing of Prof. Sanford, the book would have been impossible, and we take this opportunity to acknowledge our thanks to him. We realize, better than any one else can, the imperfections and omissions, which perhaps were unavoidable in the short time occupied in preparing this little volume, but we send it forth on its way, hoping that to some who read it may give pleasure or be of interest.   THE EDITORS.

A LAST VIEW.

MIDDLETOWN COLLEGE PATROL.
TWO-STEP

www.ingramcontent.com/pod-product-compliance
Lightning Source LLC
Chambersburg PA
CBHW030007030726
47499CB00008B/2943